Esmeralda Boyle

Songs of the Land and Sea

Esmeralda Boyle

Songs of the Land and Sea

ISBN/EAN: 9783337181864

Printed in Europe, USA, Canada, Australia, Japan

Cover: Foto ©Andreas Hilbeck / pixelio.de

More available books at **www.hansebooks.com**

SONGS

OF THE

LAND AND SEA.

BY ESMERALDA BOYLE,

AUTHOR OF " FELICE."

———✳———

New York:

E. J. HALE & SON, PUBLISHERS,

MURRAY STREET.

——

1875.

THIS VOLUME OF POEMS IS DEDICATED

TO THE DRAMATIST,

STELLA,

WHO IS A NATIVE OF MARYLAND, IN THE
UNITED STATES OF AMERICA.

CONTENTS.

———◆◆•———

Songs of the Land and Sea.

Esperanza.

[This poem was suggested by the musical sound of the word "Esperanza," as uttered by Salvini in his fervent and powerful representation of Othello.]

Along the Chilian coast wild swept the waves,
　　And lashed the shore forth reaching to the main,
Then in their lawless freedom outward rushed,
　　And dancing came again.

Borne on the air that hovered o'er the sea,
　　The scent of spice, the fragrances of flowers,
Were mingled with the odor of the brine,
　　As moments among hours.

As some fair blossom tossed upon a stream,
　　Upon the shining ocean's mighty breast
A white-winged bark moved on, and bearing down,
　　Set sail towards the west.

Oh, Western World—bright Island of the seas,
　　Outstretching from rose garlands to the snow,
And back to banks of coral, bound about
　　The South Stream's ceaseless flow !

Oh, sweet west Land, where gardens bloom and grow,
　　Low lying in the shadow of thy hills,
That hold within their moss-rimmed hearts the fonts
　　Of countless streams and rills !

Grand Western Land, by ocean breezes fanned !
　　The land first blessed by him who on thy sod
Did plant the Cross, as God's divinest mark
　　Of love to man from God !

Still sailed the " Esperanza " o'er the deep,
　　Past verdant isles and peace-inspiring ports,
Past towering cities shadowed in the sea,
　　And guarded by dark forts,

That in the lessening light of dying day
　　In strongest lines against the sky seemed set,
While ghost-like through the gloom a sentry moved
　　Upon the parapet.

A Spanish frigate, girded round with guns
    That frowned from out the ports above the tide,
And oft in salutation or in scorn
    Sent missiles far and wide,

That woke a mimic thunder on the sea,
    And from the hills brought echoes in return,
And made the vessel tremble with a thrill
    That ran from stem to stern.

She flung at length the banner of old Spain,
    With tints of mid-day wrought upon each fold,
And over all its breadth of silken pomp
    The mid-day's glowing gold.

In early days a Princess of Castile
    Had named this ship, as she herself was named,
And thus a two-fold princess on the sea
    Was " Esperanza " famed.

Swift, sailing outward to the wave-washed land,
    She left behind the promises of kings,
And gracious sunlight shone upon her prow,
    As pledge of better things.

Oh, " Esperanza," sentinel of the Main !
  Guard well the peace of fair Crescentia's shore,
Her emblem cross—her bright untarnished shield,
  As in the days of yore !

Belovéd land, that holdeth in thy clasp
  That lesser breadth of land where Calvert came
To crown thy lovely hill tops and thy meads
  With his good name and fame !

The first of every land in all the world
  Where love of God, in peace, each creed defined ;
And freedom of the heart was certified
  By freedom of the mind !

Where Christian, each, might worship as he willed,
  Where temples throning different faiths arose,
Where bigot and where martyr, side by side,
  Were shielded from their foes.

Oh, "Esperanza," sentinel of the Main !
  Guard well the peace of fair Crescentia's shore,
Her emblem cross—her bright untarnished shield,
  As in the days of yore !

The Image Breaker.

To-day, when clouds are dark and drops of rain
Fall down, to rise in misty wreaths again,
      My muse hath said,
I would make known to you in mortal phrase
A romance that I learned in fairer days
      That now are dead.

A pillared temple, reared by ancient men,
Whose minds were great beyond the common ken,
      Whose one accord
Of lofty thought, of noble purposed deed
Sprang up and grew as from the humble seed
      The forest lord,

Raised high its snowy dome, revered of Time,
Revered of Man for teachings most sublime,
      Defying wrong.
Encircled by the storm-god's tempest breath,
The temple stood through Life, from Life to Death,
      White, pure and strong.

Enshrined within its sacred marble heart
An image was, more grand than mortal art
Has since revealed,
With earnest look of faith, with form so fair,
You would have deemed some prisoned spirit there
By silence sealed.

And this was Friendship, symbolized of Truth,
Encrowned by Hope, made beautiful by Youth.
Held in her hands
A golden, burnished lamp shed lustrous light
Adown the path of pilgrims in the night
Of lonely lands.

Here friends renewed their vows, embraced and wept,
Here olden feuds were quenched, here envy slept,
Nor dreamed one dream.
Here rested those bent earthward by earth's strife,
Who lingered on the border lands of Life
Near Death's deep stream.

And thus through ages stood, and changing scene,
Unbroken and unaltered, and serene,
Through Time's increase,

The fane, the statue and the lamp of gold,
As though some magic mantle did enfold
      Their perfect peace.

One eve, when clouds of white on fields of blue,
Enwreathed with sunny rays that slanted through
      In royal dyes,
Across the path that traversed wood and plain
Came one with downcast look unto the fane
      In pilgrim guise.

Those high throned creeds by him not understood,
He hated as revilers Holy-Rood
      Or Crown of Thorns.
He held within his heart such bitter wrath
A lesser demon for some mortal hath
      He hotly scorns.

He hated that rare worker whose deep love
Shone there as shines the starlight from above
      In radiant gleams,
As trembling o'er the marble some pure thought
Beneath the chisel ran, and there enwrought
      A poet's dreams.

He hated, too, the statue carved of stone,
The regnant queen of that bright temple's throne
From ages past;
He raised his arm, he hurled it from its base,
Then fled, while Echo moaned through all that place,
Iconoclast !

The Temple quivered, swayed from side to side,
Then crashing fell, and scattered far and wide
Those marks divine
Of Love and Hope, and Peacefulness and Trust,
That lie forgotten, buried in the dust,
A broken shrine !

WASHINGTON, *April,* 1871.

THE LETTERS OF A POET TO HIS SISTER.

THE FIRST LETTER.

'Tis at the dawning of the Spring,
　　The silver gates are thrown apart,
And first of all the throng she walks,
　　The chosen princess of my heart!

Be patient, you shall hear the song
　　That wakes to music all my life;
The sweetheart poem of my youth,
　　Of one whom fate hath named my wife.

Her eyes are blue as any flowers
　　That God's eternal hands have made,
Such blooms as grow in garden lands
　　With much of sunlight, much of shade!

The smile that curves her bright red lips
　　With all of sad or tender grace,
Sends blossom tints into her cheeks,
　　And casts such glory o'er her face,

As though, while gazing toward the west,
　　Before the coming of the night,
The brightest gold the sun could give
　　Had clad her in its glowing light!

Not from her lips one word has come
　　To tell me of her days gone past,
Yet with that ken twin spirits feel,
　　I know her mine—the first, the last!

Full twenty Springs as fair as this
　　Have made a carpet for her feet,
Of greenest sward and freshest buds,
　　To ripen in the summer heat.

Her name is written by the stars,
　　When skies are clear and winds are mild,
'Tis borne upon the meadow brook
　　That seems to sing it: Edith Wylde.

The Second Letter.

Against the wiles of love your reason strikes,
    Because you have not yielded, sister mine,
Nor known the strange enthralment tyrants own,
    And call divine.

All of divinity some men may know
    Within the wide, deep scope of human life,
The love that leadeth some to peacefulness,
    Yet more to strife;

That makes some think the gates of Heaven's court
    Thrown wide to let an angel enter in,
Had let some music out upon our world
    Of shame and sin.

Yet not filled full of shame and sin is it
    Where treadeth gentle Edith. Happy space!
There shame would seem a shame unto itself,
    And sin disgrace.

Think not I note the fate that willed her birth
  In northern lands, wherein the snows lie late.
Love does not weigh each petty difference
  Of blood or state.

Your warning I acknowledge as most just,
  My judgment is not blinded by my love;
Yet all the lesser hatreds of the world
  I look above.

I fought my fight as each true soldier should,
  Our cause was lost—our hard won banner torn—
Of those who conquered us some men are true.
  The false I scorn.

Yet this fair girl, the Edith of this tale,
  Knows naught of war, of hatred nor regret;
Forgive me, dear, if through her I forgive,
  Sometimes forget.

THE THIRD LETTER.

Be sure, O sister mine! be sure
　That in her heart no thought of wrong
May, by the harshness of its notes,
　E'er mar the beauty of the song.

That song that makes her perfect life,
　The life that seems of music wrought—
The music of an inner life—
　The music of creative thought.

Nor does she stoop to worldly arts
　To add a lustre to her name;
The outer gilding weaklings crave,
　And some mistake for worth or fame.

In days agone, when Worth and Fame
　Did battle each with pen and sword,
And up the golden stairway sped
　To snatch the crown we now accord

To him who barters with that coin
  That feeds and fattens common needs,
That pays the toll to downward paths,
  And serves to stifle noble deeds—

Before this day her father's sire
  Was deemed a giant in the cause,
That lifts its stronger voice to plead
  The might and right of nations' laws.

And backward still through years of Time,
  Uplifted many a warrior face
Reveals the brow, the calm resolve
  That marks unchanged her line of race.

The calm resolve that won its way
  Against the buckler and the lance,
And wove a motto gleaming out
  Amid the lily-flowers of France.

Her father, with such claims as these,
  Holds low the praise that gold may win,
And will not enter through the gate
  Thrown wide to welcome traitors in—

Those traitors to each moral law,
  Who with unblushing faces bold,
Have choice and preference of place,
  Bought with an unjust steward's gold.

Such is the story of the blood,
  Whose current floweth through the veins
Of one who seems a very queen,
  Descended through a hundred reigns.

Each night that spreads its sombre wings,
  And every dark or shining day,
Ah, pray I follow Edith Wylde
  Till death, in her most sinless way.

The Fourth Letter.

Think not because I love her well
  That I must cease to love you, too.
You had the precedence in love
  Above the few.

As o'er the fragrances of flowers,
  . Above the sward whereon they grow,
I hear the songs of flitting birds
  That come and go.

Now that the autumn days are here,
  With leaves of scarlet, brown and gold—
The fancies of my poet heart
  In rhymes unfold.

A silver heading to each line,
  A song beginning always clear,
A melody as long as life,
  My Edith dear.

She fills my days with changeless peace,
  She brings me dreams of wedded bliss,
And yet I wonder if such joy
  Be more than this:

To see her move with native grace
  Across the lawn to where I stand,
And place within my firmer clasp
  Her perfect hand,

White as a lily rimmed with pink,
  A warmer tint within the palm;
A pulse that quickens at my touch,
  And then grows calm;

To watch the change from pearl to rose
  That mocks the dawn upon her cheeks;
To greet the smile that parts her lips
  Whene'er she speaks.

THE FIFTH LETTER.

To-day a whisper struck my heart with pain,
  Filled full of late with dreams almost divine;
Oh, send your love across this darkened space,
  Fair sister mine!

Or else for me the spring will bloom no more,
  Nor sound the summer music of the wood,
That drowns the clash of evil in the world
  And wakes the good.

I may not ask the one unnamed, to tell
  The story you may write with firmest hand,
Because your heart has never trembled, dear,
  At love's command.

Be swift to let your voice or pen reply,
  To break the thralling spell of this sad dream,
Through which the story babbles night and day
  As some wild stream

That dashes on and on adown the rock,
　And sweeps before the power of its flood
Each bright spot in its way, as a bad man
　By deeds of blood

Makes desolate the heart, and hearth and home,
　—Made beautiful with peace that dwelt therein,—
By his inhuman action taught of Cain
　And earned of Sin.

This story that to me is but half told,
　Is written in the same red blood that flows
Through her pure veins.　To you I tell the half ;
　The whole God knows.

I learn—ah, me, the pain within my heart !—
　That in the days when war debased our land,
The hand I claim was pledged.　Her hope was cast
　Upon a strand

So rugged and so barren, and so dashed
　With those wild waves that ever break and moan,
And of their bitter kisses leave the mark
　On hardest stone,

As records and as warnings written thus:
  A vessel dashed to pieces on this shore;
'Twas laden with rich ingots when it sank;
  It rose no more!

With fair white sails it wooed the summer breeze.
  With silken pennant gleaming in the sun
It broke the waves and flung caresses back
  That it had won.

Then striking on the rocks hid in the sea,
  She staggered through the darkness of the night;
The ocean roared and swept the trembling ship
  From mortal sight!

THE SIXTH LETTER.

I take it as it comes upon the wind :
   The man she loved—I may not name her name—
Had won the loyal love of a fair girl
   Ere yet he came

To blight the bloom of my fair Northern Rose,
   To sadden all the smiles upon her mouth,
To darken the bright ways that led for me
   Through our sweet South.

The other love he won was deep and warm,
   With all the summer richness and the glow
Of our dear land, gold girdled by the sun,
   Unchilled of snow !

Her name I know not. I but only know
   Her fame was fair, her heart was pure with youth.
Her face, they say, was lovely as the Spring.
   Her word was truth.

He was a man of stature tall and broad,
   His eye was dark and as an eagle's keen—
A soldier in his strength; a courtier, too,
   In voice and mien.

His name was Paul—Paul Travers—yet his name
   Is nothing, as his word of plighted trust.
No stone is on his grave. No flower grows there
   To mark the dust.

He gained the love of her I love the best.
   She wore a ring for him, and kept it bright
As armour that her fancy clad him in,
   Her soul's true knight.

Yet as her days went by, first fair and swift,
   Then darkly draped in curtaining clouds of woe,
The knowledge came by little words and signs,
   Too fast—too slow.

The Seventh Letter.

When Edith learned the faithlessness of vows
  That had been sworn, re-sworn and sworn again,
She knew her love, that might not be reclaimed,
  Was vowed in vain.

And yet, though vain, believed she still must wear
  Those chains invisible that held her slave
Against her will, to that false-hearted man,
  Whom she forgave.

For women in their weakness hold the strength
  Of something raised so high that we strong men
May strive, nor reach that height, nor understand,
  Save now and then.

Once loving, still they love, and still forgive,
  Though bowed in shame or sorrow to the dust.
The purer spirit triumphs by its force
  Of truth and trust.

Sometimes the triumph comes too late on earth
  To one who, bending low beneath the rod,
Grows weary on the way; but never late
  For grace and God.

Now, Edith proffers friendship to my love—
  That love that fain would scale the walls of Time,
To write upon the battlements of Fame
  Her name, in rhyme!

Yet think, belovéd, of her sorrowed heart!
  The anguish of her days from end to end.
No shadow half so dark, I trust, may fall
  On you, my friend.

Chilled in the radiant dawning of its hope,
  Love fettered and made captive by surprise.
A northern morning opening to the gloom
  Of winter skies!

Her brother pierced Paul Travers to the heart,
  With quick fierce thrust he rent his life in twain;
The gurgling gore that crimsoned the white stone
  Still shows its stain.

'Twas in a sheltered archway of a church,
　Near where a statue stood since early days,
With silent finger pointing up to God,
　With outward gaze.

When man to man they clutched with rivalling hate,
　And struggling fell in frenzy's unrestraint,
Upon the pavement crashed as "dust to dust"
　The marble saint.

Now send me comfort from your woman's store,
　Must I accept her friendship, tell me, Sweet?
Or shall our future, measured by her past,
　Be incomplete?

THE EIGHTH LETTER.

———

Sweet Woman-poet, Sister-love,
   The first I learned to know and prize;
Oh, frank faced girl, of tender voice!
   Oh, brown, dark eyes,

Look pity on me.   Trust me, dear.
   Forgive; and lift my heart to yours.
I as a vessel struggling out
   Leave on the shores

Glad songs, and laughter, happy homes,
   And fire-lit windows in the night,
To drift in darkness on the sea
   Bereft of light.

From Fate's full quiver kindred darts
   Speed sorrow-barbéd on their way;
One pierced my brain but yester-night,
   My heart to-day.

No knowledge that I blush to tell,
　In Edith's story I have learned.
For whom should we the blush call up,
　Where love is spurned ?

Ah, surely, surely not for her,
　My queenly Edith, fairy flower !
Whose love my love had recompensed
　With love's best dower.

Now turns my faith, my hope to you,
　Who next to God have loved me most,
Who upward led my wayward thoughts,
　A marshalled host,

To higher heights, and purer realms,—
　The land where poet's thoughts have birth.
Yet ere they plumed their golden wings
　To rise from Earth,

New born, new crowned, with songs unsung,
　A melody of you and June
Swept trembling o'er the poet's lyre,
　Half words, half tune.

3

Then you it was who, pointing up,
    Said, "Follow where the stars have led!
To God, and Truth, and love, and light,
    Tread, onward tread!"

You, with a sorrow in your heart
    Too deep for uttered word or cry,
Have bid your white despair be still,
    Your tears go by.

And holding out your hands to me,
    Oh, tender woman, sister mine!
You offer comfort born of peace
    Almost divine.

And so Paul Travers was your love?
    Paul Travers—Paul—the name that blurred
The fair white page of that sweet book
    That never erred,

In any lesson Nature taught,
    To her who wrote in purest words
The songs of streams, of sky, of wood,
    Of swift-winged birds.

You were the maid of Southern clime
  Of whom I wrote, deploring fate
That led her heart to love the man
  Whom she should hate

With all the hatred of her race,
  With all the strength of her strong kind,
With all the magnitude of heart,
  Of soul, of mind !

Nor dreamed I that with every thrust
  Your dear heart bled anew in pain,
And Memory rising crowned afresh,
  Renewed her reign.

Oh, brave, fair Woman, Sister-love,
  To you I pledge my better days,
The music of my prophet-muse,
  My harp and bays !

Echoes.

Awake, ye sleeping giants, ye
   Who lie in silence, far below
The present days that drown the sound
   Of echoes from the long-ago!

The long-ago when noble hearts
   Thought noble thoughts of noble deeds,
And lovely flowers rose and grew
   Forth from the hearts of sturdy seeds.

When all the land upheld in pride
   The loyal man of honest fame,
Whose name was honored for his acts,
   And not his actions for his name.

When something more than gold was brought
   To pave the way and grace the state
Of him who stood before the world
   And held within his grasp the fate

Of a *Republic*, staunch and true,
  That nations fain had trampled down,
Yet saved, perchance till now to writhe
  Beneath the trampling of a clown !

(I should not say that any man
  A nation's fate holds in his hand,
For He who sees each bird that falls
  Will guard the weal of our fair Land.

And some, perhaps, will stoop or fail,
  And some be faithless to their trust,
Yet He will guard our Country's weal
  Who sees the blossom through the dust.)

Awake! awake! Arouse the brave,
  The strong of heart, the pure of thought,
Who do not barter Truth for gold,
  Whose noble actions are not bought!

1861—1872.

Bold hands were prest to the strong sword-hilts,
  And white with the pallor of hate,
They fought the fight of passionate men
  In the shadow of Death and Fate.

The turf made red with the stain of blood,
  May not by the rivers of years
Be washed again to its fresh, fair tints,
  Till the sighs, the moans, and tears

Be stilled by the tranquil touch of Time;
  Till the sound of the Nation's voice
Proclaims to us in its clarion tones
  Peace! peace in the land! Rejoice!

The sunlight falls on the rose and palm,
  Yet the curse of a lawless band
Has slain fair Peace; and she wakes no more
  Love's laugh in the widowed land.

Let sweet Peace sow with a gracious will,
  Over hill and valley and plain,
The ripened seed of a loyal trust
  That will grow to shining grain.

From the shores that wreathe the Southland gulf,
  From the peaks of the icy North,
The startled cry of a nation's heart
  To the nations rushes forth!

From rocks that woo the Atlantic's kiss,
  From Pacific's wild, free slope,
Rings the cry for Peace from souls of men
  Near the goal of a people's hope!

THE YEAR OF PROMISE.

The Year of Promise breaks its way
    Into the fold of Space and Time,
And loudly ring its matin bells,
    And all its golden lyrics chime!

The Past that flits so far away
    Through memory's mist is scarce discerned,
Yet ere she went, her smiling face
    Towards the Promised Year she turned.

And all the radiance of her gaze,
    And all her hope went out and bound
In perfect love the hearts of those
    Who for the Promised Year are crowned.

With such sweet peace as is their meed
    With all such pure and lovely things,
As make good women like to queens,
    And honest men seem more than kings.

1873.

A Dream of the Stars.

I dreamed that some stars in heaven,
　Beclad in a flood of light,
Were ranged as the hosts of battle
　On the field of blue, for fight.

They sped with the speed of meteors,
　And the rays like golden bars
Broke through, on the fields of azure,
　The ranks of the lesser stars.

Some stars in the mystic struggle
　Grew pale in the strife and fled.
They hid in the clouds their faces,
　Their light to the world was dead.

Yet some through the night went flashing,
　As a bird through ether darts,
We clasped our hands and awaited
　With fear of God in our hearts.

When the dream of Life is broken,
   When the roll of Time shall cease,
Will stars in the sky thus herald
   The Prince of the House of Peace?

January, 1874.

The Sugar Loaf Mountain.

Afar the giant Mountain rose to view,
And out and up our purer feelings grew
      To something good ;

And dark as are the shadows of Despair,
The shadows lying long and darkly there
      On rock and wood.

Yet from the placid sky with azure spread,
Upon the kingly crest, the royal head,
      The sun shone down,

As though a spirit band that hovered near
Had left upon that peak for love or fear
      A golden crown.

And softly slid the sunlight from that place,
Till, lost among the shadows at the base,
      It broke and fled

In tiny flakes of light, in mellow rays,
Like cherished thoughts of sweet, departed days
　　　That are as dead.

We climbed up to the fearful demon's den,
A throng of fair-faced women, stalwart men,
　　　With jest and song.

Far, far beyond our bandit-like retreat
Potomac ran, a bright, wild love to meet,*
　　　Then sped along.

An Indian maid, with rare, untutored grace,
Bearing her chieftain's arrows to the chase,
　　　Swift, swiftly on!

From rock to rock a stone before us flashed,
Then wandering Echo moaned, as down it crashed,
　　　Forever gone!

No, not forever gone; though rudely tossed
From thy grand, rocky height, thou art not lost.
　　　On plain and hill

* Monocacy.

With other atoms thou wilt bind the world,
Although, perhaps, unknown, through darkness
    hurled,
        A white stone still.

Yet, looking with the eyes of fond Romance,
We see thee raised, in later days perchance,
        From thy dim home,

To deck some mosaic pavement of the mart,
Some pillared temple reared by modern art,
        Some palace dome!

Adown the cliffs, the crags, the rock-bound ways,
Still droops the Summer's crowning wreath of bays
        O'er brake and glen;

And from the kiss of breezes free and wild,
Looks up the fern, the mountain's well-loved child,
        From cave or fen.

And far above the clash and worldly din,
Ah! far beyond its earthly dust, its sin,
        Are peaceful nooks:

A tranquil home for some stern, conquered chief,
Whose cause is lost, who seeks a last relief
   In prayer—or books.

Far, floating o'er our heads, in ether dim,
We saw birds whirl—are they more near to Him
   For lifted wings?

Ah! not so near, although they seem more near!
Ah! not so dear, as we to Him are dear
   Beyond all things.

Down, down we wound, and from the vale at last
Looked back, as through Life's sorrows to the Past
   Our hearts behold

The ways that lead from pride of birth or state
—The little world decrees, its fear, its hate—
   Through gates of gold.

The air was fresh with rain that fell at noon,
The hamlet showed, though silvered by the moon,
   Its ancient mode.

A drowsy silence lingered there, most sweet,
As if some olden spirit walked the street
        Where it abode

In earth-life days, of strength and bravest deeds,
Ere Freedom's Queen had donned her sable weeds
        For fallen Truth—

Ere haggard Vice and Mammon stalked the land,
And beckoned on to Hell with withered hand
        Our country's Youth!

Out-rang our song, " Good-bye," perchance for aye;
No, we will drive that tearful thought away
        Forever more!

Here is to Hope, the beautiful, the true!
Our hearts are thine, we pledge our faith anew,
        Encore! encore!

MONTGOMERY Co., MD., *August* 29*th*, 1871.

"LOVE ME LITTLE, LOVE ME LONG."

"Love me little, love me long,"
  Through the spring-time rain and sun,
Through the might of Right and Wrong,
  When the days of youth are done.

In the Noontide's glorious glow,
  When the Evening mounteth high,
On her throne of gleaming snow
  In her pageant robes to die,

With pink flushes on her cheek,
  With gold arrows in her hand,
Pointing upward to each peak,
  Where her marshalled armies stand;

When the rose has lost its bloom,
  When the leaves are dropping down,
In the Autumn's purple gloom,
  On the grasses sear and brown;

When the Bird shall fold its wings,
   And in silence hold its song,
With that peace the Twilight brings,
   " Love me little, love me long."

March 22*d*, 1874.

4

The Place of Dreams.

Far over the limits of Race and Time,
Runneth a river in rarest rhyme.
    Along the shore
Is a Country, peopled not overmuch,
That claimeth and holdeth only such
    As know its lore.

Its wonderful Temple, that pointeth high,
In silvery curtainings of the sky,
    Is half-way lost.
With glorious jewels of flashing fire
Forth from each white, celestial spire
    Are banners tossed.

There are beautiful birds that now and then
Float up from the crowded Land of Men,
    Into that world,
To gather the songs that trembling there,
Sail slow on the languid mid-day air,
    That seems impearled

In a marvelous mist of gold and blue,
Where odors of violets wafted through,
Are stirred by the birds of the swiftest wing,
That gather the notes of songs of Spring
     For mortal ears.

And these are the sighs and the heart-wrung
     moans
That sink into chords of tender tones,
     And ripple to tears.
And these from a soul's ungained desire,
Sweep from the strings of a poet's lyre
     Through lapsing years.

Now uttering brief—now lingering long,
In unlearned measures of untaught song,
     Their peace or pain.
Thus borne are our thoughts to the shell-rimmed
     shore,
The Palace of Poets, whose open door
Leadeth us in from the Place of Dreams,
Where wandereth out from musical streams
     That which is heard
     In the voice of a bird :

The pæans it snatched from the far off land,
Of turrets and domes, where the singers stand,
Who wear unchanged the immortal crown,
Kingliest, queenliest, Just Renown!

Washington, *D. C., Nov.,* 1875.

The Days that are not Yet.

Before us lie rare summers rich with roses,
  And thrilled with water-music not yet heard.
Hark! just as day glides thro' the pale of twilight,
  A sweet voiced bird

Sings out its song that slides into the silence—
  Then all the shining leaves upon the trees
Dance, and a sound like laughter or swift clapping
  Comes on the breeze.

Above our path the white moon glides beyond us,
  And clouds make fleeting shadows as they pass,
And in the mellow light the crystal dew-drops
  Gleam on the grass,

As though an eastern princess or a fairy,
  With lips that smile, with eyes that darkly frown,
Had cast on hill and glade a jeweled sceptre,
  A zone, a crown.

O, Time, unborn! so sweet in future story!
  As sweet as are these days of sun and rain,
Sweet as past days that our fond hearts in dreaming
    Seek out again!

The days that are not yet in light or shadow,
  May give us sleep beneath the grass ungrown,
Graced by some plant with leaflets yet unmoulded,
    With blooms unblown.

September 8, 1872.

THE KNIGHTS OF THE GOLDEN HORSE-SHOE.

With the clang of the hoofs of horses
    The vales and mountains rang,
And borne on the breeze of the summer,
    Were songs the soldiers sang.

In the shade of the leaf-clad branches,
    Beneath the shielding blue,
As the green leaves quivering parted,
    Bright rays went sliding through.

Through the reeds of the wind-swept meadow,
    By gray old cliffs and crags,
Where the blossoming pink of laurel
    Waved like a thousand flags,

A stream with the gleam of a sabre
    Fled through the wood and grass,
As a loud, free laugh in the echo
    Breaks through a mountain pass.

And on, on through the dew-dashed shadows,
    Full loud the soldiers sung,
And clear on the air of the morning
    The sound of horse-hoofs rung.

And the same sweet air that in blowing
    Had brushed the rose's bloom,
Now swept o'er the brow of the leader,
    And touched his scarlet plume.

In the days of valorous glory,
    Heeding his soul's behest,
He fought in the fight at Blenheim,
    Fought with a knightly zest!

Ah! brave heart of the Old Dominion!
    * Chief, and maker of laws,
In the van of the grand old legions,
    Gone with the chosen cause!

* "Alexander Spotswood, a soldier who had been wounded at Blenheim. Under his leadership the mountains were crossed, and the beautiful valleys beyond were made known. On his return he presented to each of the companions of his journey a golden horse-shoe."—[*Holmes's History*.

Yet as bold as my wilful fancy,
　　Back from the times of yore,
And into this dream of the summer
　　Those who have gone before

Wind down from the peaks to the meadow,}
　　Beyond the stalwart trees,
Where the sun-lighted *guidon* flutters,
　　Stirred by the morning breeze.

With the clang of the hoofs and armour
　　The vales and mountains ring,
And borne on the breeze of the summer
　　Are songs the soldiers sing.

September 18, 1872.

ABAFT THE BINNACLE.

Abaft the binnacle sat the boy,
   And over the waves of ocean blue
His gaze was fixed, and I knew his heart
   Led over the waves and out to you.

Across his face swept ever the tide
   Of dreamy thought, to the days agone,
And by the light in his deep dark eyes
   I knew of the spell that led him on.

The night came down with a fiend-like storm,
   A fiery flash and a shrieking wind,
And following on like a serpent's trail
   The gleam on the sea we left behind.

The morning broke with a deadened calm,
   With tattered sails and a shattered mast;
We steered our course to the distant land,
   And left the storm in the blackened Past.

The boy was gone from the staunch old deck,—
 In the serpent trail of the ship's broad wake,
That chased us down through the fearful night,
 His soul rushed out ere the morning's break.

Only this picture I sketch for you,
 Who stirred his life with a strange, wild joy;
That while his heart sailed over the sea
 Abaft the binnacle sat the boy.

June 4, 1874.

My Sweetheart Muse.

The summer has touched with her wand of gold
    The blades of wheat,
That ripple and sway in the breeze that breaks
    The noontide heat.
Through the shadowy lanes that upward lead
    From glen and dell,
As the loitering kine stroll slowly home,
    We hear the bell
That ringeth a peal on the air, made sweet
    With falling dews,
And wooeth her out of her castle high,
    My sweetheart-Muse;
Who glideth forth at the close of the day,
    With look serene,
In amber and rose, with silver girt,
    A crownéd queen.
Sweeter than life is the love we give
    And never obtain.
Sweeter than life the hopes we hope,
    Although in vain.

Yet sweeter than earthly hope or love
    The one I choose
To walk in the path of life with me,
    My sweetheart muse !

MARYLAND, *June* 12, 1874.

To the South.

My free wild Love, I love thee!
　Fair as the sun-gold's shine!
Bright is the sky above thee,
　O, free wild love of mine!

Strong with the strength of valor—
　Graced with a knightly grace.
First in the lists of battle—
　First in the world's high place!

Oh, brave, fair Love, we greet thee—
　Land of the mighty life!
Land of the soul of sorrow!
　Land of the chosen strife!

Heart of the rushing river!
　Home of the wild-wood lord!
Land of the silent soldier!
　Land of the faithful sword!

Land of the " Conquered Banner !"
  Land of the rose and vine !
Bright is the sky above thee,
  Thou free wild love of mine !

March 7th, 1875.

A Legend of the Christmas-tide.

Full high on the rounded hill tops,
　　Deep, deep in the valleys below,
And over the Queen's grand garden
　　Was falling the feathery snow.

In the still white marble palace,
　　And as pure as the snow that fell,
The weary soul of a woman
　　Was wearily sighing farewell;

Where, scattered in strange confusion,
　　There were silks and jewels and lace,
That glared with a pale cold lustre
　　Through gloom, in that sorrowful place.

From the rare bright silks and jewels
　　The dying one turned to depart,
Her heart in their clasp was breaking,
　　Ah, what were they now to her heart!

Death shades were drearily flitting—
   Flitting over her face full fair;
A priest in his robes was kneeling—
   An old priest with silvery hair.

Opened the door of the chamber
   Widely—wide with a noiseless swing—
There entered a rag-clad beggar—
   A beggar who trod as a king;

And these are the words he uttered:
   "Behold, I have come through the storm!
You gave me bread when I hungered,
   And you clothed me and made me warm!"

The priest with the hair like silver
   Looked up, but the vision had fled;
He knelt alone in the chamber
   Where the woman was lying dead.

Yet down through the great, sad silence
   Came the chords of a harp's gold strings,
The sweep of invisible garments,
   And the rustle of angel wings.

THE BROKEN FEAST.

Ah, the chimes of merry Christmas
    Ring out gaily on the breeze,
Yet the feasts that I remember
    Were more beautiful than these!

All the grandeur we could gather,
    Every treasure we could bring,
We did cast before the altar
    Of Emanuel, the King.

Like the rushing sound of pinions,
    In the land where all is fair,
Was the throbbing of the music
    As it beat against the air.

* Bathed in semblance of the moonlight
    Were the pictured hills and sward,

---

* It is a custom in Catholic countries to erect during the Christmas-tide representations of the manger. These picturesque nooks are adorned with miniature rocks, moss-banks and trees. Figures of

And the manger where the princes
  Knelt in homage to our Lord.

And, when at the solemn warning
  Every knee was bended low;
Ah! we felt that God was near us
  In His robes as white as snow.

It was thus He taught the fishers,
  As their teachings all are told,
And our hearts believe those teachings,
  As the fishers did of old.

Now, forever and forever
  Comes the memory to me
Of the music that I hear not,
  For the sobbing of the sea;

And as moaning, mournful billows,
  With their sad and ceaseless roll,
Are the longings that go outward
  To the country of my soul.

hovering angels and kneeling shepherds are gathered in groups.
Thus are Catholic children taught of the coming of the *Royal Redeemer*, as others are taught to honor soldiers and statesmen through
monuments and "legal" public holidays.

Hold thy peace, young Roman rebel !
  Wherefore weep, Italian child ?
Rather laugh above the shackles
  That did make thy land defiled !

Lo ! the conqueror has conquered,
  And no greater lives than he ;
Now rejoice with all thy people
  That fair Italy is free !

In the soft and dreamy cadence
  Of the master-poet's clime
Spake the youth in lowly murmurs,
  And his face was made sublime :

I was reared within the shadow
  Of the *ancient church at Rome,*
Whence I saw the evening sunlight
  Fling its gold upon the dome ;

And this cross that I am wearing
  Is the cross my mother wore
When the army of King Victor
  Swept before our cottage door.

God's bright sun was shining on us,
　On the cross its glory flashed,
And a soldier stooped to snatch it
　As the troopers onward dashed.

Then, as with a new won courage,
　Down I struck his coward arm.
Pale, like marble, stood my mother
　In her womanly alarm.

Then my father, the staunch guardian
　Of our home-loves and our hearth,
With the fierceness of a lion
　Hurled and crushed him to the earth!

Now, it seemed a dozen vandals
　Joined them in one traitor's part—
Sent their deadly sabres flashing
　To my father's noble heart.

So he died, and just beside him
　Fell my mother's stately form,
Then the soldiers fled and left us.
　There are clouds before the storm!

Ah, if this dark woe be freedom
  That has wrought our lives such pain,
Give us back the chains of bondage
  That will make us slaves again!

Yes, the chimes of merry Christmas
  Ring out gaily on the breeze,
Yet the feasts that I remember
  Were more beautiful than these.

WASHINGTON, D. C., *December*, 1872.

I Fain would Enter In.

I heard the moaning wind beat on the wall;
  It made the tender twigs and dead leaves fall;
It rushed from door to casement with its din;
  It seemed to say, " I fain would enter in—
    Thee I implore !"
Yet, though the wind blasts o'er the heath were
    hurled,
  The calm, queen-moon was reigning o'er the world;
The moonlight past the leafless branches crept,
  And through the clear, cold panes in silence swept
    Down to the floor.

" I fain would enter in," by night and day
  Sings Sin, the beautiful, in fair array.
We open out our soul's close-barréd gate,
  Then enters the long train: First, Pride elate,
    With visage bold;

Last, dark-browed Envy comes, unsatisfied;
  Forever crying, " Open wide, more wide !

We will not part with thee through Life's great
    space ;
  Deny us not thy soul's most sacred place
    To have and hold."

"I fain would enter in," our Lord doth say,
  "To still thy sobs, to chase thy tears away—
To lull thy aching heart in perfect rest;
  Ah, lay thy weary head upon my breast!
    I am the Son,
Sent down as a Redeemer to the earth,
  Who, in a lonely manger-crib, sought birth ;
Crowned, heart and brow, with thorns, for wayward
    men,
  And died upon a rough, hard cross—what then,
    Beloved one ?"

July, 1873.

The Good Old Christmas.

And so the good old Christmas comes again!
  The merry Christmas of our vanished years;
With all its tender beauty and its mirth,
      Its silent tears.

Green with the fair remembrances of youth,
  And garlanded with hopes of better days;
Those olden mottoes of the Christmas-tide,
      Filled full with praise.

Filled with the praiseful voices of the spring,
  The murmuring streamlets of the summer glade:
Oh, Christmas days of sorrow and of joy,
      Of sun, of shade!

Filled full with red and gold of autumn tints,
  Filled with the ice-glints of a Northern clime;
Oh, ghosts of gone-by Christmases, recall
      The olden time!

The olden time of purer thoughts and ways,
   The olden time of purer words and songs,
When men at holy Christmas-tide undid
     Their baleful wrongs.

The wrongs that murder love, and peace and fame,
   The wrongs that turn man's friendship into hate;
The wrongs that make forgiveness and regret
     To plead too late;

Too late for that poor heart they broke in haste—
   Late for the life that may not come again—
Yet not too late for God, whose charity
     Is as the rain,

Plenteous and refreshing, and most good,
   And beautiful as silver in the sun!
Or bright as is an angel's diadem
     For victories won!

November, 1875.

"The Master is Come and Calleth for Thee."

The Master is come and calleth for thee
Across the grain-decked field, the barren moor !
List ! For He knocketh at the palace gate,
      The cottage door.

He speaks to thee in Wisdom's golden tongue,
From children's lips He calls to thee again :
" Let not my coming here be welcomeless,
      Nor yet in vain !

" In royal robes I stand, on marble floors,
With kingly hands stretched forth I call to thee,
Wait not the coming night—the trumpet's sound
      To rise and flee !

" Now while the morning is—before the night
Falls darkling o'er the dust of utter dearth,
Rise thou and follow. Make thy garments clean
      From stain of earth !

" With thorn-pierced brow upturned I plead to thee,
I wait in lowly places for thy alms !
With aching heart, with lingering weary feet,
   With nail-torn palms !"

" The glory of the Son forever is !"
We hear the angels singing far away,
As they draw near to portals opening out
   From inner day.

Wait thou ! wait thou ! His coming is not far.
He loves thee well ! The step of love goes swift,
O lids that droop, O eyes made dim in tears,
   Uplift ! Uplift !

Uplift thine eyes ! Ah, see the Light is come !
Uplift thine heart ! nor let thy heart hold tears.
He comes to thee adown the narrow vale
   Of blighted years !

Arise, thou dreaming ones, and watch with us,
Lest in the vaults of death thy lamps grow dim :
Up narrow ways, that lead from Death to Life,
   Go wait for him.

 May 2, 1874.